Pete the Cat

and the Missing Cupcakes

To all of Pete's friends everywhere.
Matthew 6:14
—J.D. & K.D.

ISBN 978-1-338-33008-3

Text copyright © 2016 by Kimberly and James Dean. Illustrations copyright © 2016 by James Dean.
All rights reserved. Published by Scholastic Inc., 557 Broadway, New York, NY 10012,
by arrangement with HarperCollins Children's Books, a division of HarperCollins Publishers.
SCHOLASTIC and associated logos are trademarks and/or registered trademarks of Scholastic Inc.

12 11 10 9 8 7 6 5 4 3 2   18 19 20 21 22 23

Printed in the U.S.A.   40

First Scholastic printing, September 2018

The artist used pen and ink with watercolor and acrylic paint on 300lb press paper to create the illustrations for this book.
Typography by Jeanne L. Hogle

Pete the Cat
and the Missing Cupcakes

Kimberly and James Dean

SCHOLASTIC INC.

Pete and Gus were as busy as could be.
They were getting ready for the cupcake
party. It started at three!

They were making cupcakes for everyone.
Pete and Gus counted them just for fun!

They had ten when they were done.

OH NO! HANG ON!

Some of the cupcakes were gone!
They were sure there had been ten.

Pete said, "Maybe we need to count again!"

They counted the cupcakes
lined up straight.
Now there were only eight!

It looked like someone had taken two.

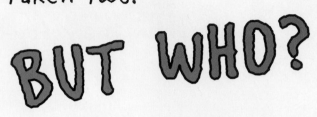

Pete and Gus did not know what to do!

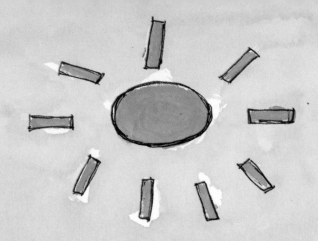

Just then they found a clue.

Gus said, "Look what I have found. Sprinkles on the ground! I bet it was Squirrel. She loves sprinkles."

Squirrel said,

"It wasn't me!
It couldn't be!
I've been at the spelling bee!"

"Uh-oh. More cupcakes are missing. Come and see!"

THIS WAS TOO WEIRD!

Two more cupcakes
had disappeared!

Now there were only six!
Someone must be playing tricks!

BUT WHO?

Pete and Gus did not know what to do!

Just then they found
another clue!

Pete said, "I bet it was Alligator!
He loves to eat."

Alligator said,

"It wasn't me!
It couldn't be!
I've been learning my ABCs!"

"Uh-oh. More cupcakes
are missing. Come and see!"

Now there were only four!
Someone had taken two more!

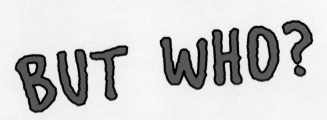
BUT WHO?

Pete and Gus did not know what to do!
Just then they found another clue.

"I bet it was Turtle," said Pete.
"I know Turtle loves sweets."

Turtle said,

"It wasn't me!
It couldn't be!
I've been swimming in the sea!"

"Uh-oh. More cupcakes are missing.
Come and see!"

What on earth was going on?
All the cupcakes were now

GONE!

Pete and Gus did not know what to do!

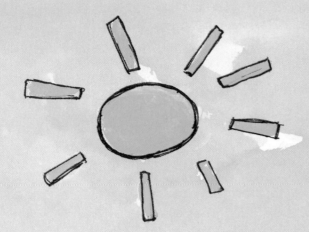

They started looking for
another clue.

They found Grumpy Toad with icing
on his face!
Pete and Gus have solved the case.

Everyone agreed—Grumpy Toad would
have to miss the fun.
He could not come after what he had done.

Pete said, "But wait! Grumpy Toad made a mistake. This is true. Let's give him a second chance. That's what friends do!"

Pete told Grumpy Toad they would give him another chance.
He was so excited. He did a happy dance!

The night of the party was so much fun. Grumpy Toad brought more than enough cupcakes for everyone!

Katie McGee

In 2004, **Kimberly & James Dean** sat down at their kitchen table to work on a children's book together. Their dream finally became a reality with the release of *Pete the Cat and His Magic Sunglasses*. Both left corporate jobs in the late nineties (James was an electrical engineer; Kimberly worked in the press office of the governor of Georgia) to pursue their passion for art, and they have experienced a life made up of strange and wonderful coincidences ever since. Pete the Cat has brought magic into their lives. They work in side-by-side studios in Savannah, sharing their home with five cats and Emma the pug.